Dear Parent:
Your child's love of reading starts here!

Every child learns to read in a different way and at his or her own speed. Some go back and forth between reading levels and read favorite books again and again. Others read through each level in order. You can help your young reader improve and become more confident by encouraging his or her own interests and abilities. From books your child reads with you to the first books he or she reads alone, there are I Can Read Books for every stage of reading:

SHARED READING
Basic language, word repetition, and whimsical illustrations, ideal for sharing with your emergent reader

BEGINNING READING
Short sentences, familiar words, and simple concepts for children eager to read on their own

READING WITH HELP
Engaging stories, longer sentences, and language play for developing readers

READING ALONE
Complex plots, challenging vocabulary, and high-interest topics for the independent reader

ADVANCED READING
Short paragraphs, chapters, and exciting themes for the perfect bridge to chapter books

I Can Read Books have introduced children to the joy of reading since 1957. Featuring award-winning authors and illustrators and a fabulous cast of beloved characters, I Can Read Books set the standard for beginning readers.

A lifetime of discovery begins with the magical words **"I Can Read!"**

Visit www.icanread.com for information
on enriching your child's reading experience.

THE HIGH AND THE FLIGHTY

Time Warp Trio created by Jon Scieszka

Adapted by Catherine Hapka and Lisa Rao

Based on the television script by Peter K. Hirsch

HarperCollins*Publishers*

Time Warp Trio™ is produced by WGBH in association with Soup2Nuts for Discovery Kids.
HarperCollins®, ▆®, and I Can Read Book® are trademarks of HarperCollins Publishers.

Library of Congress catalog card number: 2006929490
ISBN-10: 0-06-111644-0 (trade bdg.) — ISBN-13: 978-0-06-111644-5 (trade bdg.)
ISBN-10: 0-06-111643-2 (pbk.) — ISBN-13: 978-0-06-111643-8 (pbk.)

Typography by Joe Merkel
1 2 3 4 5 6 7 8 9 10

First Edition

CONTENTS

Meet the Time Warp Trio:

Three girls from the twenty-second century with a taste for adventure.

The Book

The Book looks like a book, but acts like a time machine. The girls can use it to go anywhere in history, but they have to be careful. If they change anything in the past, the future could change, too. And the girls need to remember: If they lose *The Book*, they can never get back home.

The Girls

Jodie: A popular kid. Her great-grandfather Joe gave *The Book* to her.

Samantha: A smart kid. She likes to solve mysteries.

Freddi: A loyal kid. Her friends love her.

CHAPTER 1

Flying High and Falling Fast

"You did it," Freddi says to Jodie.

"You put us on the Electra!"

Freddi, Jodie, and Samantha

just warped onto

Amelia Earhart's plane.

Jodie coughs.

"Too bad I couldn't warp us

into first class.

This plane smells of gas."

The three girls look out the window.

The plane is diving downward!

CHAPTER 1 1/2

From Airwaves to Airborne

It all started with
Samantha's old radio.
It was a gift from Samantha's
great-grandfather.
Sometimes Samantha's radio
picks up signals from long ago.

This was one of those times.
The radio picked up a distress call
from Amelia Earhart.

Amelia Earhart became
famous in the 1930s.
She was the first woman
to fly across the Atlantic Ocean.
Her plane was lost over
the Pacific Ocean in 1937.
Nobody knows what happened to her.

The girls decided to warp back to 1937
to answer Amelia's distress call.
"But no messing with history,"
Jodie warned.
Jodie opened *The Book*.
Green mist poured out.
It swirled around them.
Then the girls were gone.

CHAPTER 2
Just Plane Scary

Back in the plane, the girls are scared.

The plane is going to crash!

But Amelia is at the controls.

She stays cool and

guides the Electra

safely to the ground.

Amelia thinks the girls are just fans who stowed away on her plane.

The girls are glad.

But that feeling doesn't last long.

Jodie realizes *The Book* is missing.

The girls search the Electra

for *The Book*.

Samantha finds something interesting.

It's a map of the Pacific Ocean.

She knows Amelia flew over it on her

final flight.

Then she notices something
even more interesting.
There is a big red X on the map!
"Whoever made this map
knows where the plane
is going down," she cries.

Samantha finds a signature
on the map.
The name of the mapmaker
is Fred Noonan.
Fred is Amelia's navigator.
Could he be planning
to hurt Amelia?

Drafted by
Fred Noonan

"Got it!" Jodie cries.

She finally found *The Book.*

Just then a man walks in.

His name is Stu.

He works for a magazine.

He wants to find shocking things
to write about Amelia.

And he's willing to pay for them.

CHAPTER 3
Car Trouble

The girls ignore Stu

and his money.

They think they may have solved

history's biggest mystery.

Maybe they can save Amelia.

(So much for not messing

with history.)

The girls rush to Amelia's house.

They spot her car.

Then they see her legs sticking

out from under it.

"We're too late—she's DEAD!"

Freddi cries.

Meanwhile, Stu is watching

the girls' every move.

But Amelia is alive and well.

She was just working on the car's engine.

Jodie tosses *The Book* into the car.

Then she tells Amelia about the map.

Amelia doesn't believe

that Fred would plot against her.

Just then Jodie notices something.

The Book is gone—again.

She jumps into the car to search for it.

CRE-E-E-EAK!

The car starts rolling downhill

with Jodie inside it.

Samantha and Freddi run after
the car and jump in to save Jodie.
But the car picks up speed.
None of them can jump out.

And that's not the scariest part.

A plane is roaring right toward them.

"AAAAAHHHHHHH!" the girls

scream.

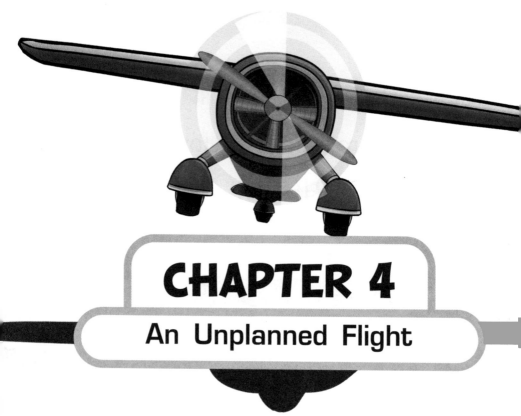

CHAPTER 4

An Unplanned Flight

Luckily the plane takes off
before it smashes into the girls.
But they're not safe yet.
The car is still speeding downhill . . .
toward the airplane hangar.

Samantha figures out what to do.

She tells her friends her plan.

It's their only chance.

When the plane is right overhead,

Jodie grabs the wheel bar.

The others hold on to her legs.

The girls fly high into the air.

The girls are out of the car,
but they're still in big trouble.
"I'm slipping!" Freddi cries.

Meanwhile, Amelia is nearby.

She sees the car crash into the hangar.

Then she sees the girls

hanging on to the plane.

She knows what she must do.

She jumps into another plane,

and flies to the rescue.

She catches the girls

just as they lose their grip.

Soon the girls are
back on the ground.
Amelia has saved the day!
But they're still worried
about that red X on the map.
They think Fred Noonan
has some explaining to do.

But when Freddi tells Fred and Amelia about the map, they just laugh.

The X stands for Howland Island.

"It's where we have to land to refuel," Fred says.

The girls haven't solved the mystery. . . and *The Book* is still missing.

CHAPTER 5

Feeling Stu-pid

The next day the girls watch

as Amelia prepares to take off.

Freddi tries to warn her
about what will happen.
She doesn't want Amelia to crash.
But Amelia is brave.
"Have a good day, girls," she says.
"I know I will."

The girls look around
for *The Book*.
They still can't find it.

But they do find a
copy of Stu's magazine.
Jodie reads the headline out loud:
"'Amelia Earhart is a Martian.'"

Samantha looks at the picture.

"*The Book* is in this photo," she cries.

"That reporter must have it."

Stu must've grabbed *The Book*

from the car when they weren't looking.

The magazine article says

Stu will sneak onto Amelia's plane.

If Stu stows away on the Electra,

he will go down with the plane.

And so will *The Book*.

And if *The Book* is destroyed,

the girls will never get back home.

They rush outside.

CHAPTER 6

Far Out

Amelia's plane is about to take off.

Freddi runs after it.

She tells Amelia to search the plane.

At first Amelia is annoyed.

But then she finds Stu and kicks him out.

Stu does have *The Book* . . .
but he won't give it back.
Then Samantha has an idea.
If they convince Stu they
are Martians, maybe he'll be
scared and give back *The Book*.
"Amelia's not a Martian,"
Samantha says, her eyes wide.
"But we are, ightray, Odiejay?"

The three girls start talking in pig latin.

Then Samantha pulls out her radio.

"What's that?" Stu asks.

He sounds kind of scared.

Jodie tells him it's a space phone.

"She's using it to call

the mother ship," she says.

"Maybe we should bring
Stu home with us," Jodie says.

"Yes," Samantha agrees.

"A gift from planet Earth."

"Wait a minute!" Stu yells.

That's when Freddi jumps forward
and grabs *The Book*.

"Hey," Stu cries.

He realizes they've tricked him.

"You just wanted your book back.

You're not Martians."

"Are you sure?" Jodie asks.

She flips open *The Book*.

CRACK!

The girls disappear in a flash.

CHAPTER 7

History Mystery

Samantha and Jodie are happy

to be back in the future.

But Freddi can't stop

thinking about Amelia.

She wonders if Stu was the one

who made the plane crash.

Now that they stopped him,

maybe Amelia would be safe.

"Let's see if Amelia made it
around the world,"
she tells her friends.

They open *The Book*.

"Here we go..." Jodie says.

"'Amelia Earhart, born 1897.

Lost over the Pacific, 1937...

plane wreckage never found.'"

Freddi can't believe it.

Nothing has changed!

They still don't know what
happened.

"It's a mystery, and that's
the way it's going to stay,"
Jodie says.

"Maybe some mysteries
aren't meant to be solved,"
Samantha adds.

Freddi thinks Jodie may be right.
Some mysteries just aren't
meant to be solved. . . .

THE END

AMELIA EARHART: THE PLANE FACTS

Amelia Earhart was born in Kansas, in 1897. When she was ten years old, she saw an airplane for the very first time at the Iowa State Fair. Amelia later said the airplane was "a thing of rusty wire and wood and looked not at all interesting." But in 1919, Amelia went to watch a stunt-flying exhibition with her dad. She decided planes weren't as boring as she first thought!

Amelia took her first flying lessons at Kinner Field, near Long Beach, California. Her teacher was Anita Snook, a pioneer female aviator. Six months later, Amelia bought her first plane, a bright yellow biplane she called Canary.

Soon Amelia's dreams of flight were as big as the sky. On October 22, 1922, she flew Canary to an altitude of 14,000 feet, setting a women's world record.

In 1932, Amelia became the first woman to fly solo nonstop across the Atlantic Ocean. Among many other awards, she received the Gold Medal of the National Geographic Society from President Herbert Hoover for her achievement.

Amelia's last flight took place in 1937. Her goal was to fly all the way around the world at the equator. But it was not to be. Amelia and her navigator, Fred Noonan, disappeared close to the end of their mission. What became of them remains a mystery to this very day.